For Geraldine, Joe, Naomi, Eddie, Laura and Isaac
M.R.

For Elaine, Charlotte and Nicola
A.R.

Aladdin Paperbacks
An imprint of Simon & Schuster
Children's Publishing Division
1230 Avenue of the Americas, New York, New York 10020
Text copyright © 1990 by Michael Rosen. Illustrations copyright © 1990 by Arthur
Robins. All rights reserved including the right of reproduction in whole or in part in
any form. LITTLE SIMON and colophon are trademarks of Simon & Schuster. Also
available in a SIMON & SCHUSTER BOOKS FOR YOUNG READERS hardcover edition.
Manufactured in Hong Kong
20 19 18 17 16 15 14 13 12
ISBN 0-671-79604-6

Little Rabbit Foo Foo

Retold by Michael Rosen
Illustrated by Arthur Robins

Aladdin Paperbacks

Little Rabbit Foo Foo

riding through the forest,

scooping up the field mice

and bopping them on the head.

Down came the Good Fairy
and said, "Little Rabbit Foo Foo
I don't like your attitude,
scooping up the field mice
and bopping them on the head.
I'm going to give you three
chances to change, and if you
don't, I'm going to turn you
into a goonie."

Little Rabbit Foo Foo
riding through the forest,

scooping up the wriggly worms
and bopping them on the head.

Down came the Good Fairy

and said, "Little Rabbit Foo Foo,
I don't like your attitude,
scooping up the wriggly worms
and bopping them on the head.
You've got two chances to change,
and if you don't, I'm going to
turn you into a goonie."

Little Rabbit Foo Foo
riding through the forest,
scooping up the tigers
and bopping them on the head.

Down came the Good Fairy
and said, "Little Rabbit Foo Foo,
I don't like your attitude,
scooping up the tigers
and bopping them on the head.

"You've got one chance left to change,
and if you don't, I'm going to
turn you into a goonie."

Little Rabbit Foo Foo
riding through the forest,
scooping up the goblins

and bopping them on the head.

Down came the Good Fairy
and said, "Little Rabbit Foo Foo,
I don't like your attitude,
scooping up the goblins
and bopping them on the head.

"You've got no chances left, so I'm
going to turn you into a goonie."